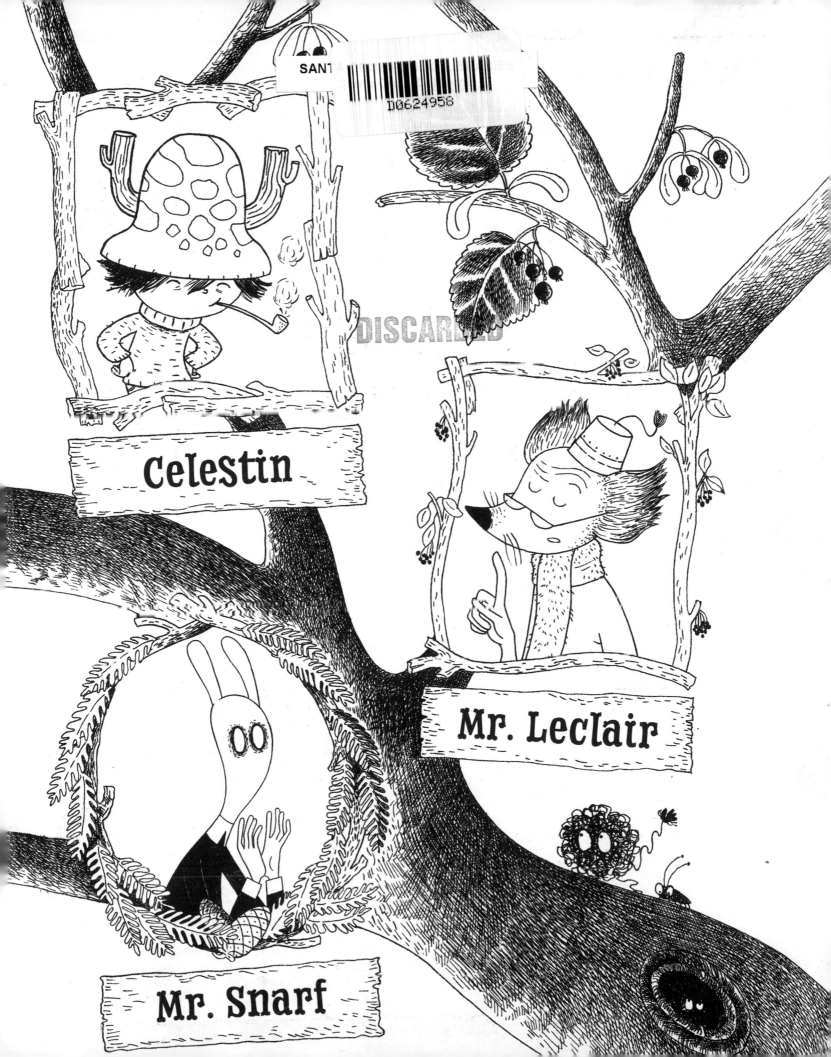

Celestin

Mr. Leclair

Mr. Snarf

HOTEL STRANGE

Wake Up, Spring #1

Florian and Katherine Ferrier
illustrations and coloring by Katherine Ferrier

Graphic Universe™ • Minneapolis

Story by Florian and Katherine Ferrier
Illustrations and coloring by Katherine Ferrier
Translation by Carol Burrell

This work received the support of La Cité internationale de la bande dessinée et de l'image (comics museum, library, and arts complex) through an author residency at La maison des auteurs in Angoulême, France.

First American edition published in 2015 by Graphic Universe™

Copyright © 2010 by Sarbacane, Paris
published by arrangement with Sylvain Coissard Agency in cooperation with Nicolas Grivel Agency

Graphic Universe™ is a trademark of Lerner Publishing Group, Inc.

Graphic Universe™
A division of Lerner Publishing Group, Inc.
241 First Avenue North
Minneapolis, MN 55401 USA

For reading levels and more information, look up this title at www.lernerbooks.com.

Main body text set in Andy Std 11/12. Typeface provided by Monotype.

Library of Congress Cataloging-in-Publication Data

Ferrier, Florian, author.
    Wake up, spring / by Florian and Katherine Ferrier ; illustrations and coloring by Katherine Ferrier ; translation by Carol Burrell.
        pages cm. — (Hotel Strange)
    Summary: Although it is spring, the winter weather will not end and the quirky residents of Hotel Strange decide to find out for themselves where Mr. Springtime has gone.
    ISBN 978-1-4677-8584-6 (lb : alk. paper)
    ISBN 978-1-4677-8648-5 (pb : alk. paper)
    ISBN 978-1-4677-8855-7 (eb pdf)
    1. Graphic novels. [1. Graphic novels. 2. Seasons—Fiction.]
I. Ferrier, Katherine, author, illustrator. II. Burrell, Carol Klio, translator. III. Title.
PZ7.7.F48Wak 2015
741.5'973—dc23   2015000711

Manufactured in the United States of America
1 – VP – 7/15/15

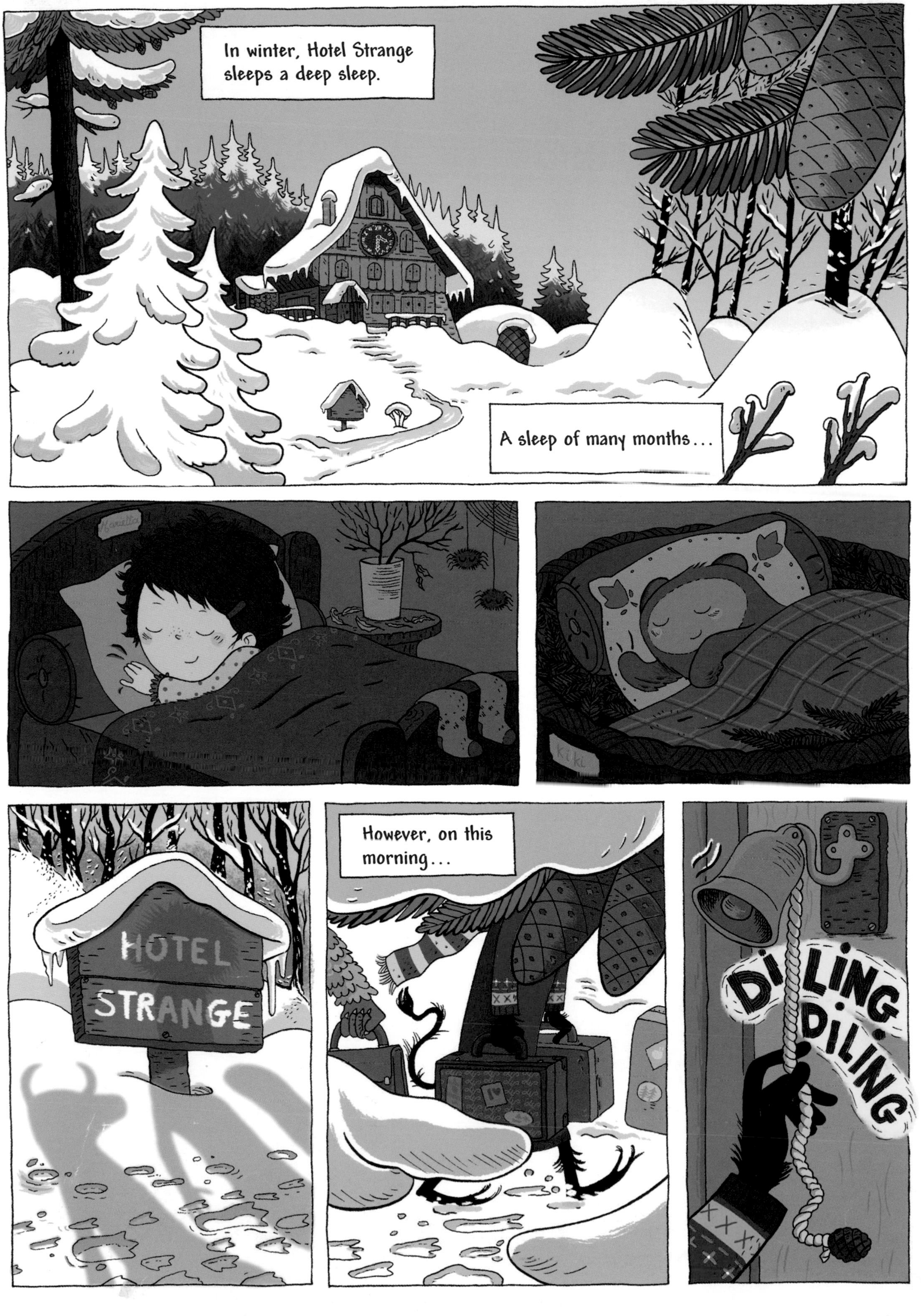
In winter, Hotel Strange sleeps a deep sleep.
A sleep of many months...
HOTEL STRANGE
However, on this morning...
DiLING DiLING DiLING

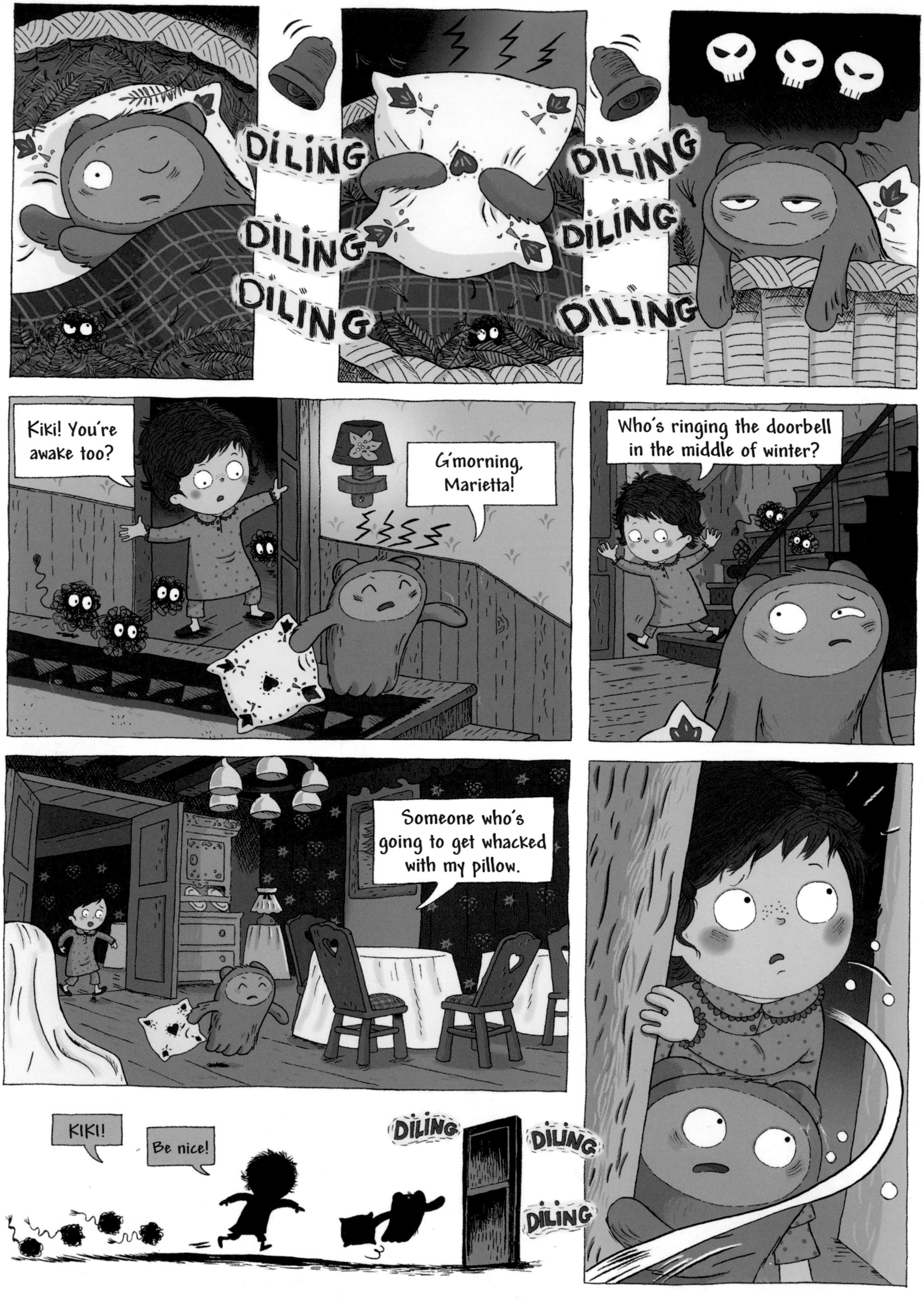
DILING
DILING
DILING
DILING
DILING
DILING
Kiki! You're awake too?
G'morning, Marietta!
Who's ringing the doorbell in the middle of winter?
Someone who's going to get whacked with my pillow.
KIKI!
Be nice!
DILING
DILING
DILING

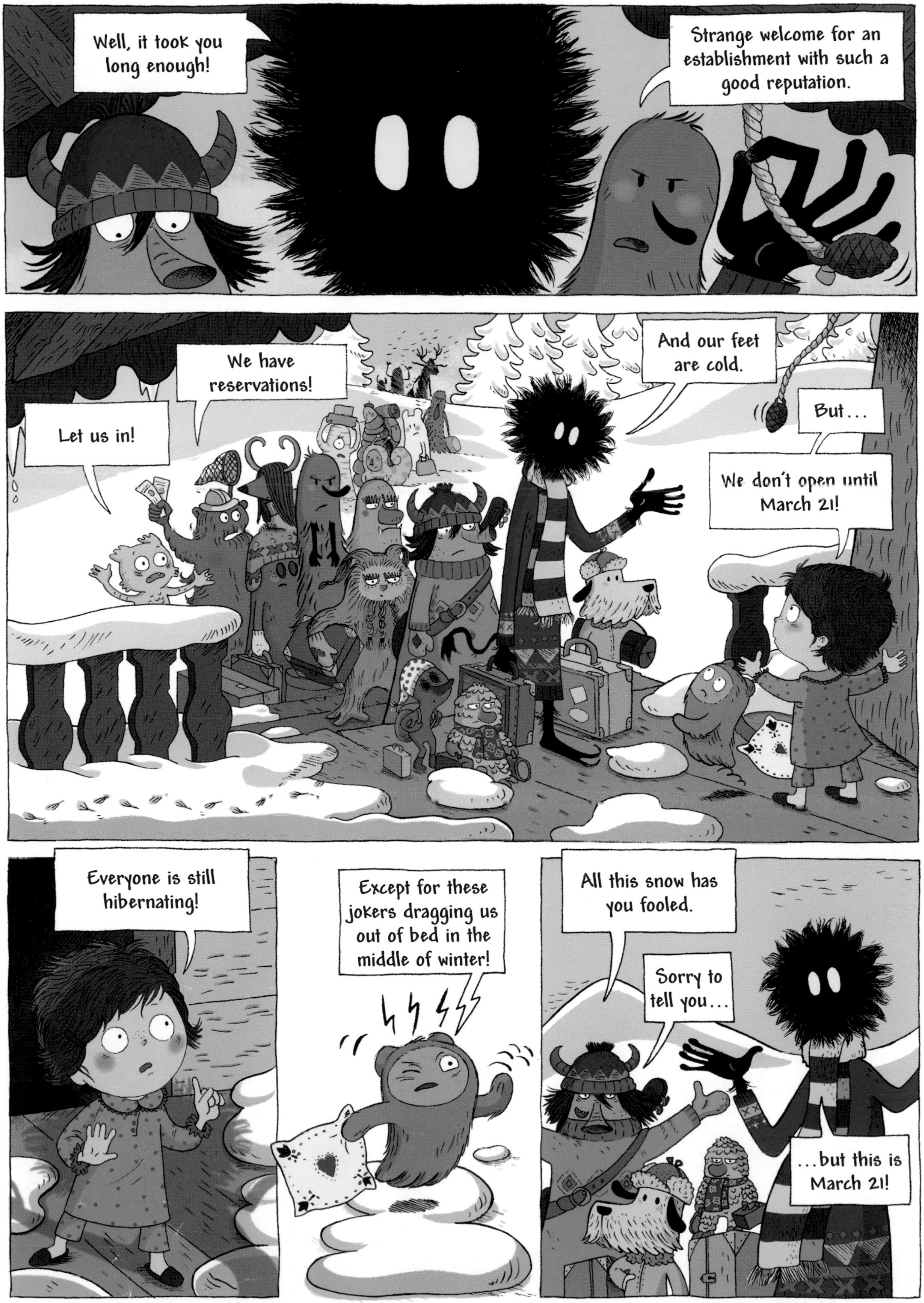
Well, it took you long enough!
Strange welcome for an establishment with such a good reputation.
Let us in!
We have reservations!
And our feet are cold.
But...
We don't open until March 21!
Everyone is still hibernating!
Except for these jokers dragging us out of bed in the middle of winter!
All this snow has you fooled.
Sorry to tell you...
...but this is March 21!

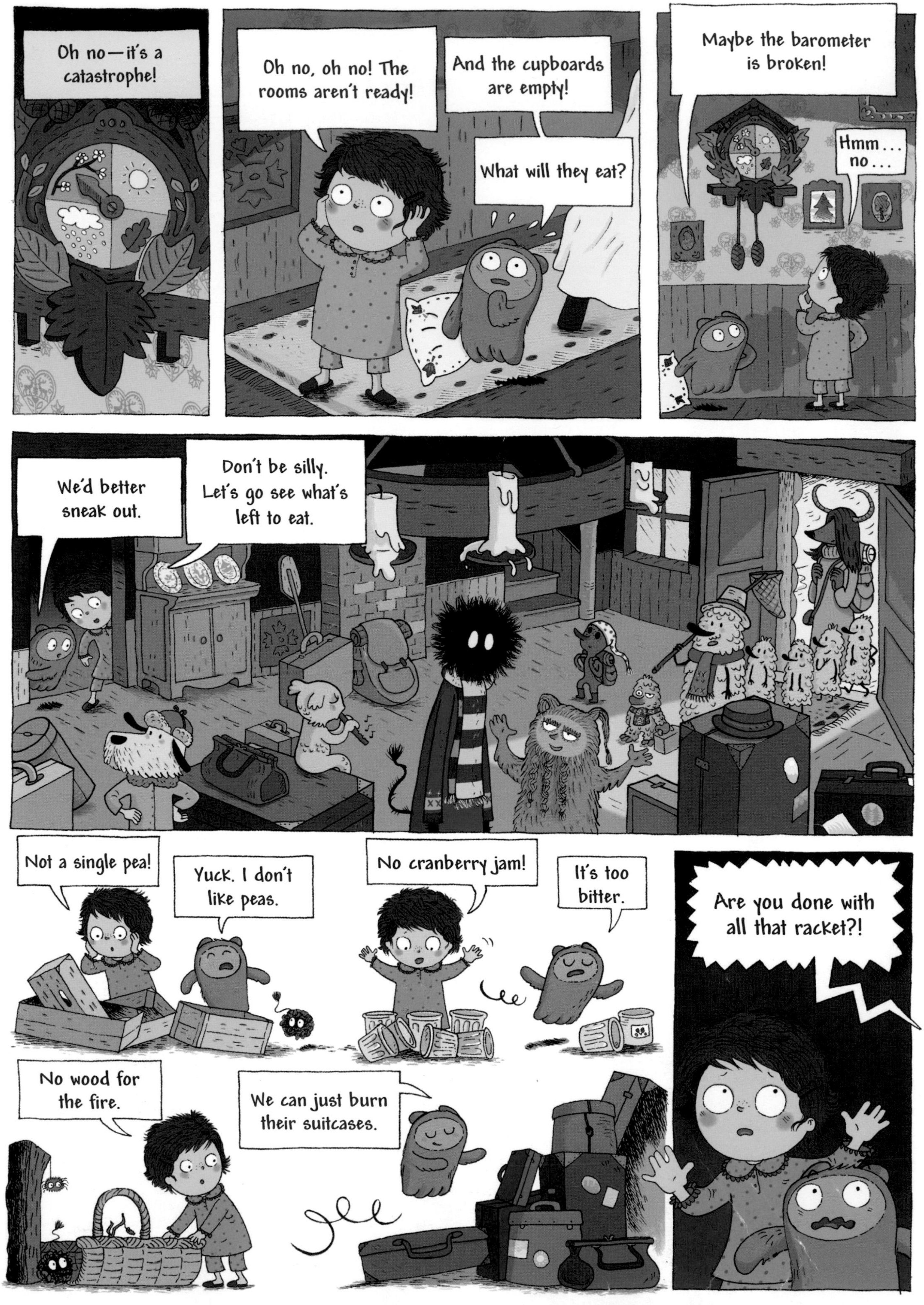
Oh no—it's a catastrophe!
Oh no, oh no! The rooms aren't ready!
And the cupboards are empty!
What will they eat?
Maybe the barometer is broken!
Hmm... no...
We'd better sneak out.
Don't be silly. Let's go see what's left to eat.
Not a single pea!
Yuck. I don't like peas.
No cranberry jam!
It's too bitter.
No wood for the fire.
We can just burn their suitcases.
Are you done with all that racket?!

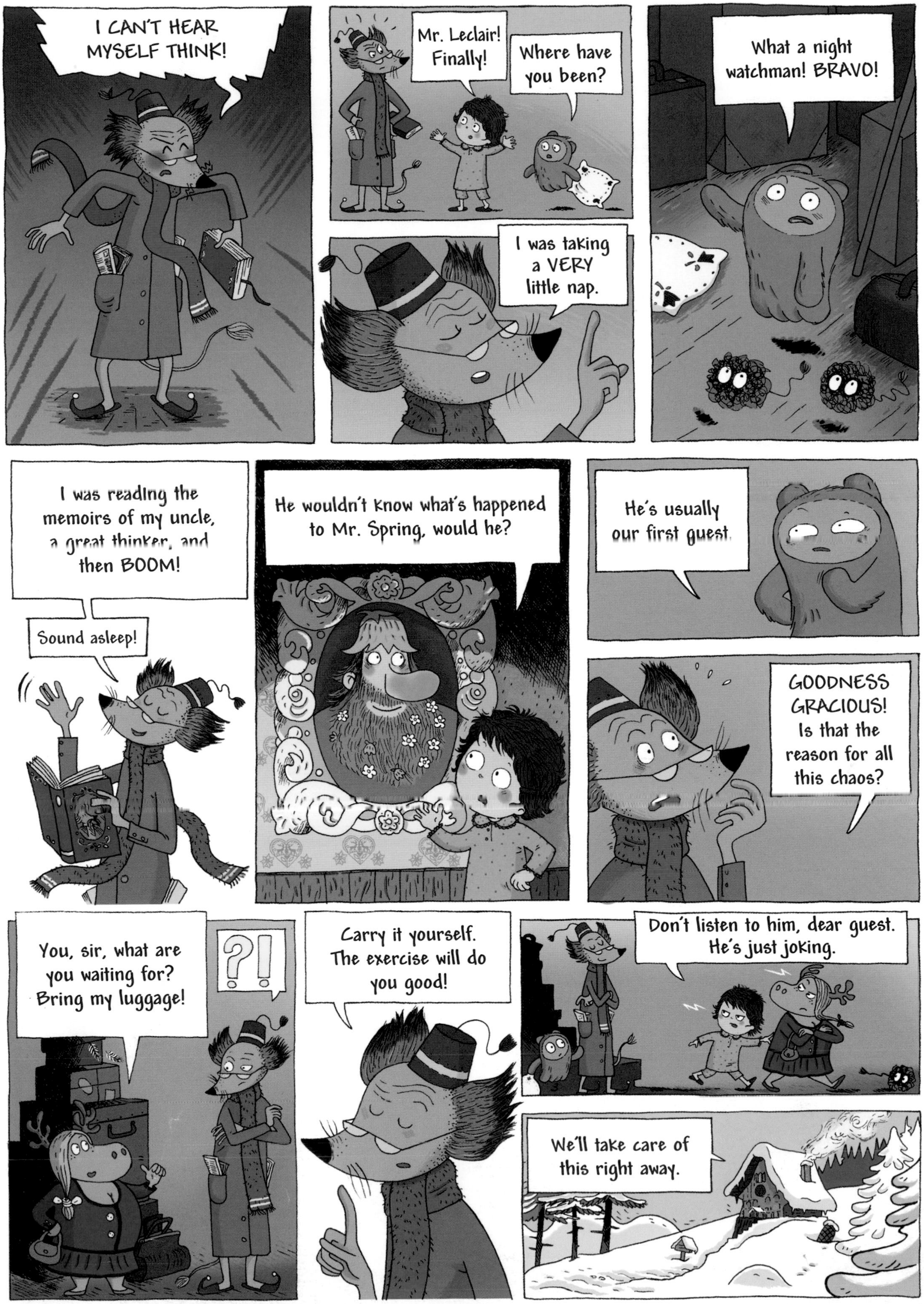
I CAN'T HEAR MYSELF THINK!
Mr. Leclair! Finally!
Where have you been?
I was taking a VERY little nap.
What a night watchman! BRAVO!
I was reading the memoirs of my uncle, a great thinker, and then BOOM!
Sound asleep!
He wouldn't know what's happened to Mr. Spring, would he?
He's usually our first guest.
GOODNESS GRACIOUS! Is that the reason for all this chaos?
You, sir, what are you waiting for? Bring my luggage!
?!
Carry it yourself. The exercise will do you good!
Don't listen to him, dear guest. He's just joking.
We'll take care of this right away.

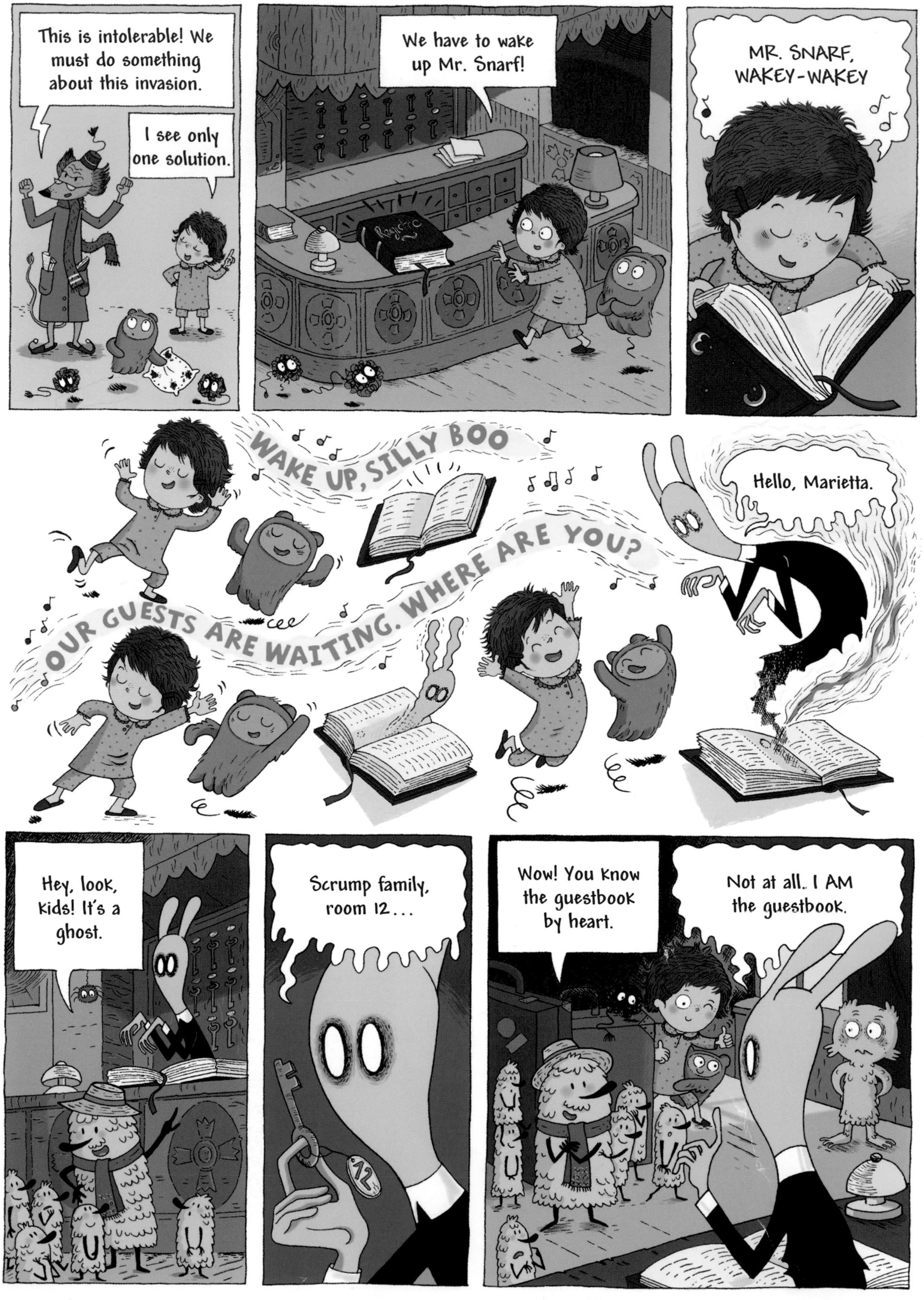
This is intolerable! We must do something about this invasion.
I see only one solution.
We have to wake up Mr. Snarf!
MR. SNARF, WAKEY-WAKEY
WAKE UP, SILLY BOO
OUR GUESTS ARE WAITING. WHERE ARE YOU?
Hello, Marietta.
Hey, look, kids! It's a ghost.
Scrump family, room 12...
12
Wow! You know the guestbook by heart.
Not at all. I AM the guestbook.

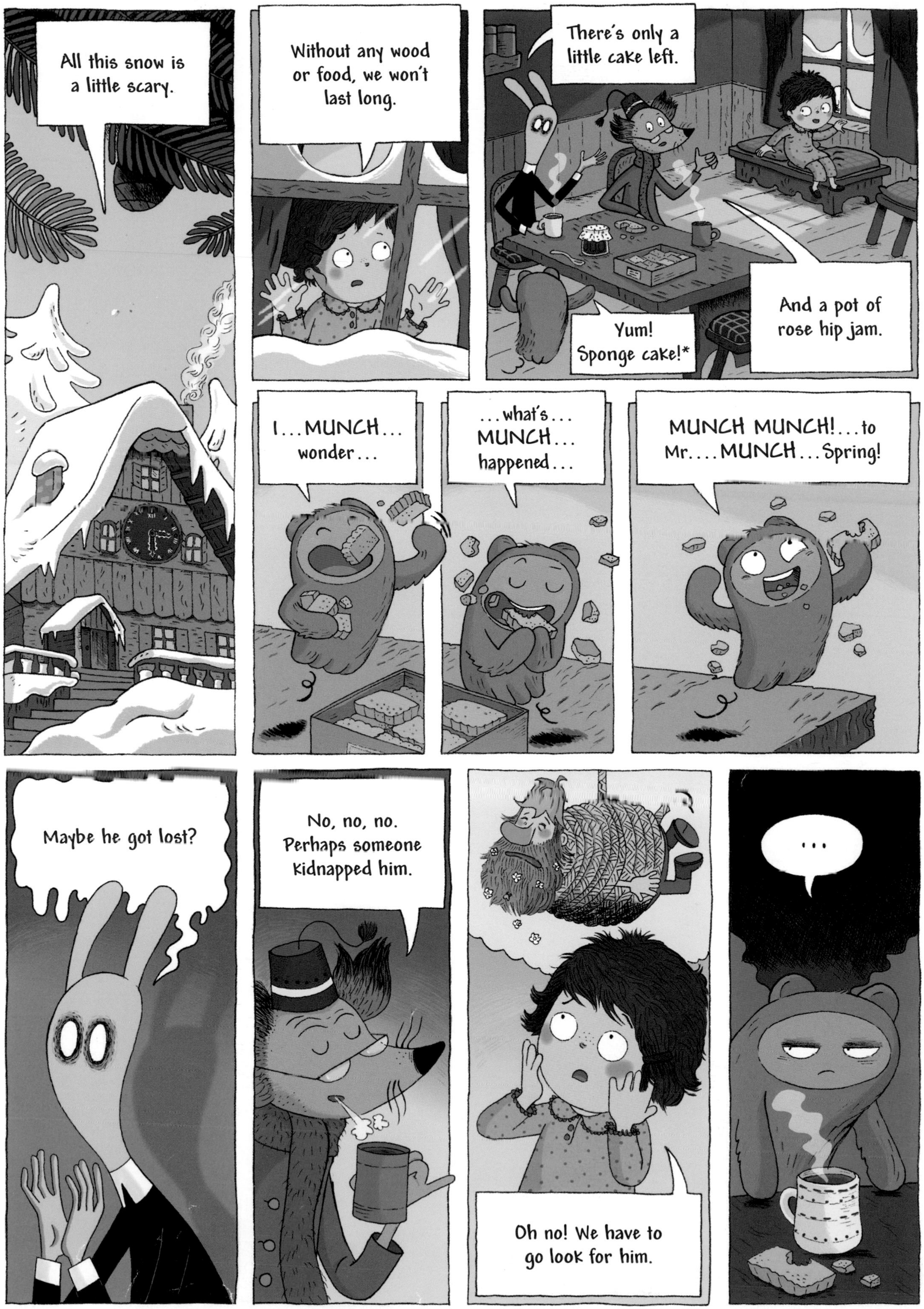
All this snow is a little scary.
Without any wood or food, we won't last long.
There's only a little cake left.
Yum! Sponge cake!*
And a pot of rose hip jam.
I... MUNCH... wonder...
...what's... MUNCH... happened...
MUNCH MUNCH!... to Mr.... MUNCH... Spring!
Maybe he got lost?
No, no, no. Perhaps someone kidnapped him.
Oh no! We have to go look for him.
...

*See the SPONGE CAKE recipe at the end of the book!

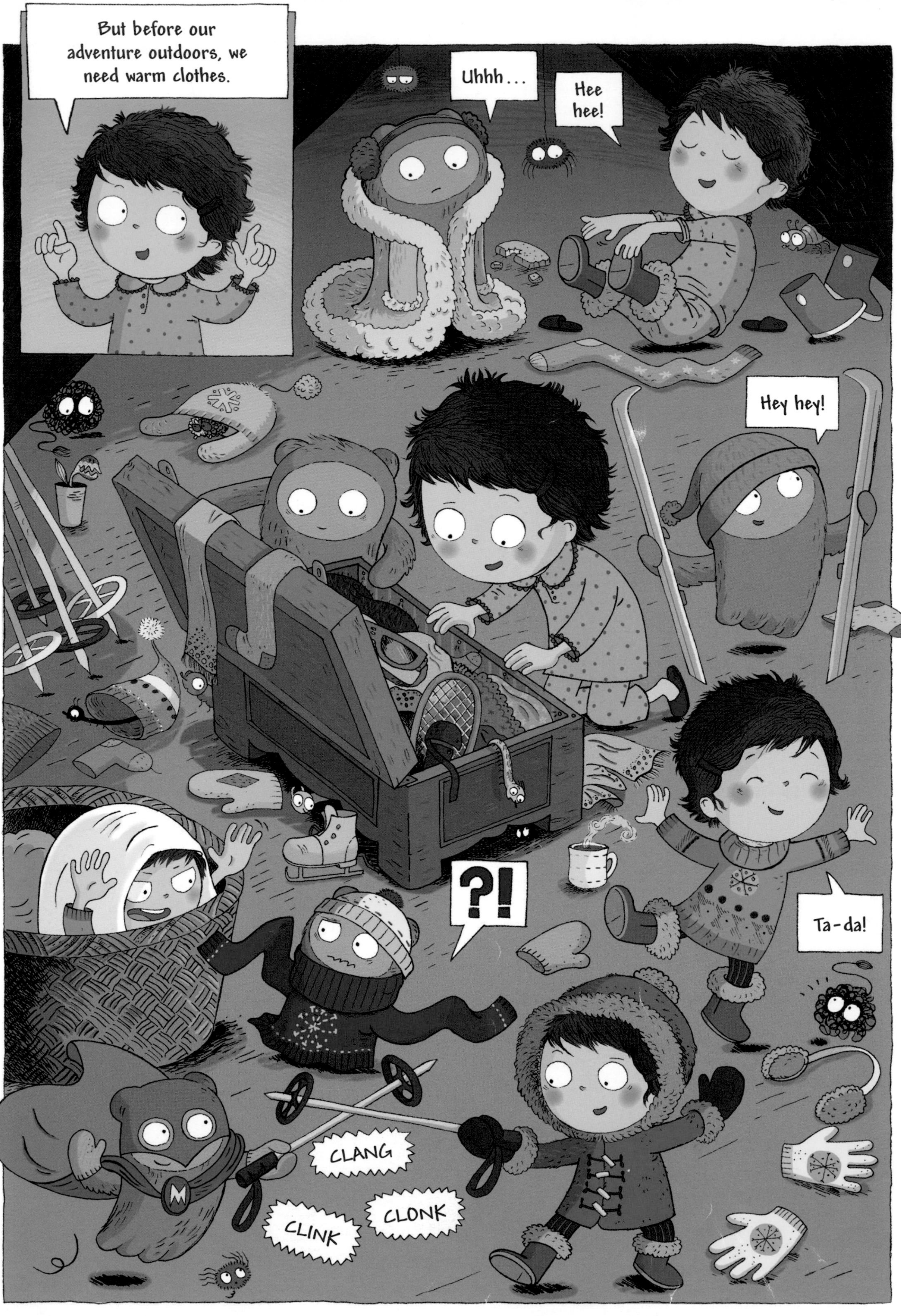

But before our adventure outdoors, we need warm clothes.
Uhhh . . .
Hee hee!
Hey hey!
?!
Ta-da!
CLANG
CLONK
CLINK

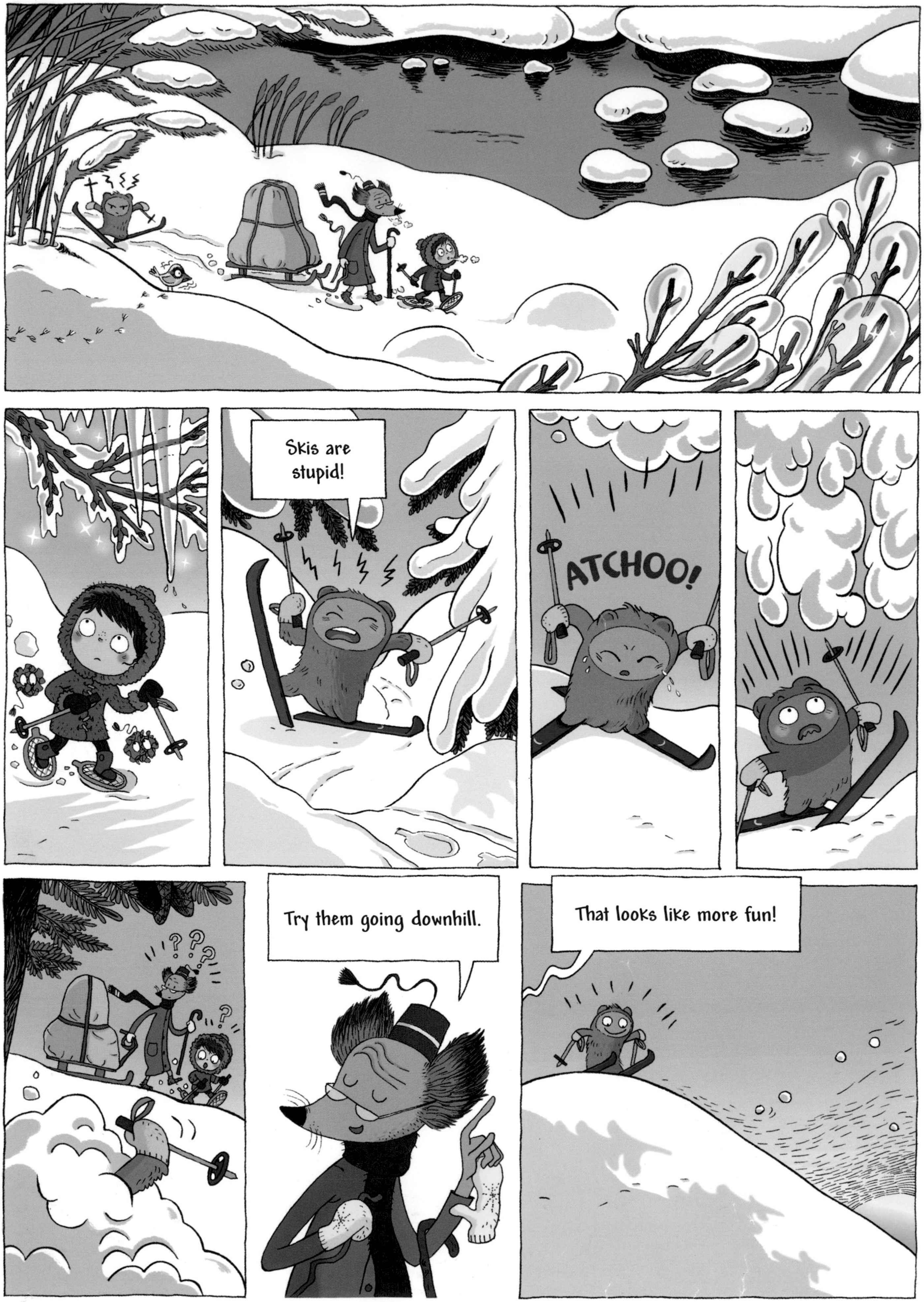
Skis are stupid!
ATCHOO!
Try them going downhill.
That looks like more fun!

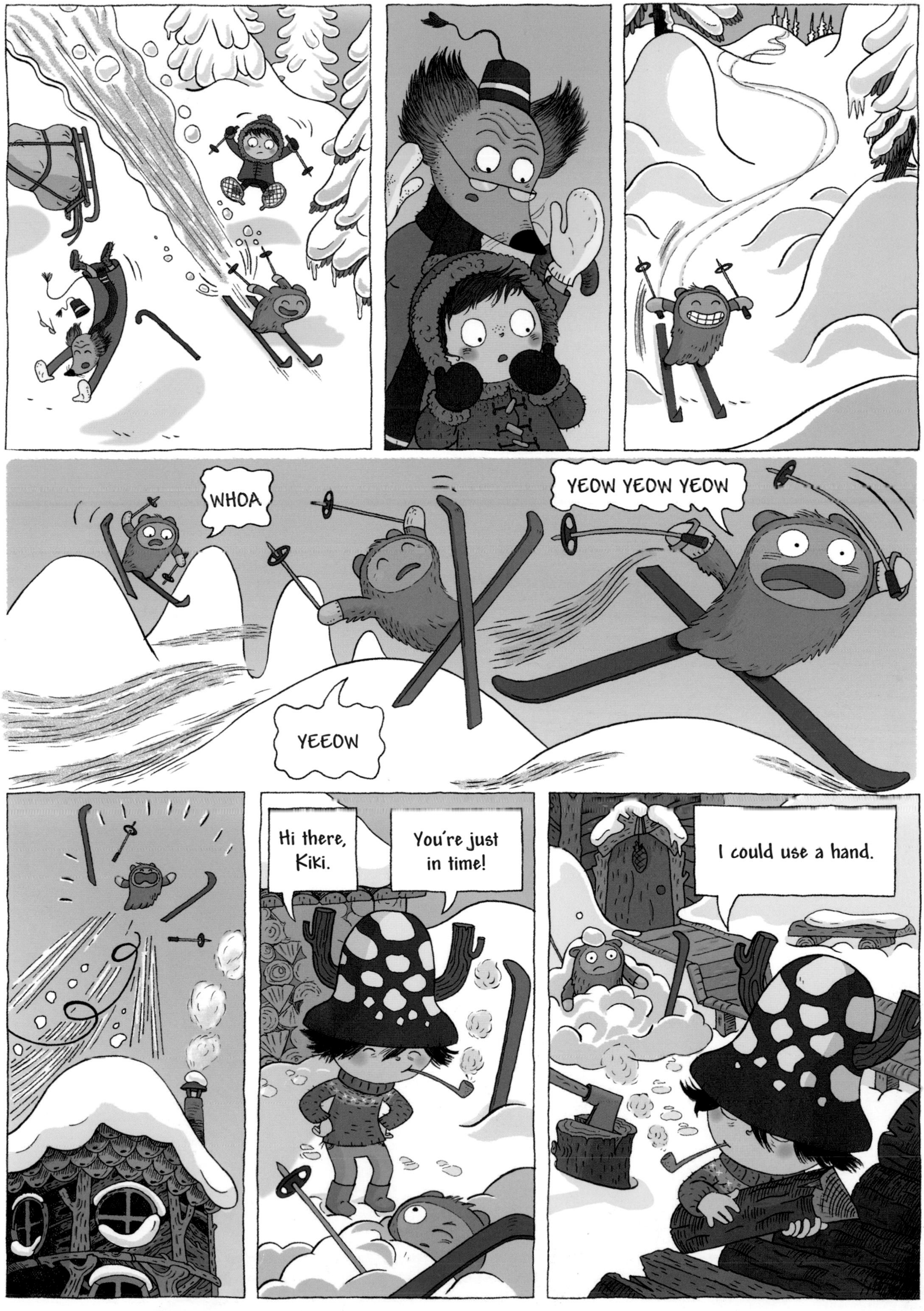
WHOA
YEOW YEOW YEOW
YEEOW
Hi there, Kiki.
You're just in time!
I could use a hand.

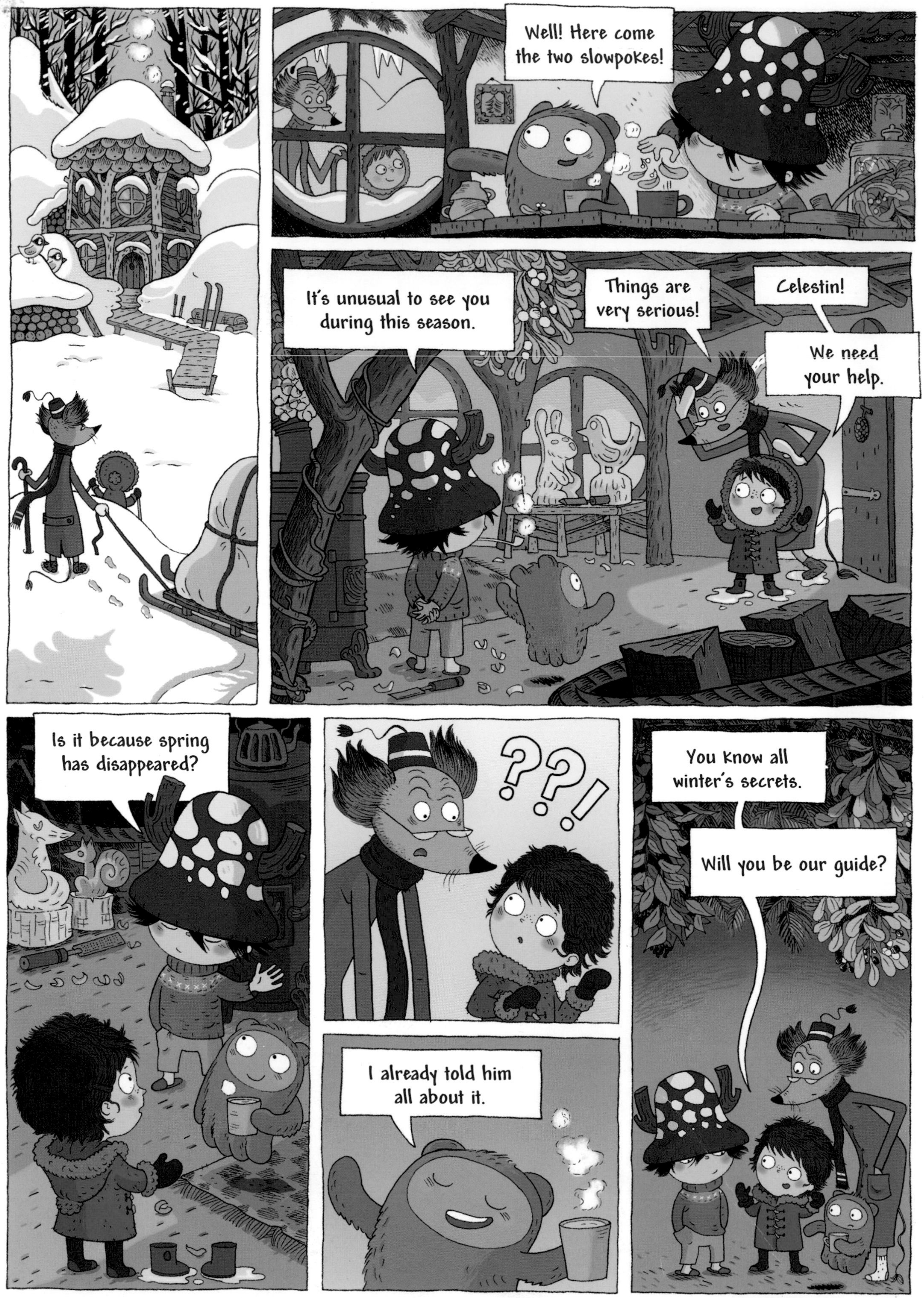
Well! Here come the two slowpokes!
It's unusual to see you during this season.
Things are very serious!
Celestin!
We need your help.
Is it because spring has disappeared?
??!
I already told him all about it.
You know all winter's secrets.
Will you be our guide?

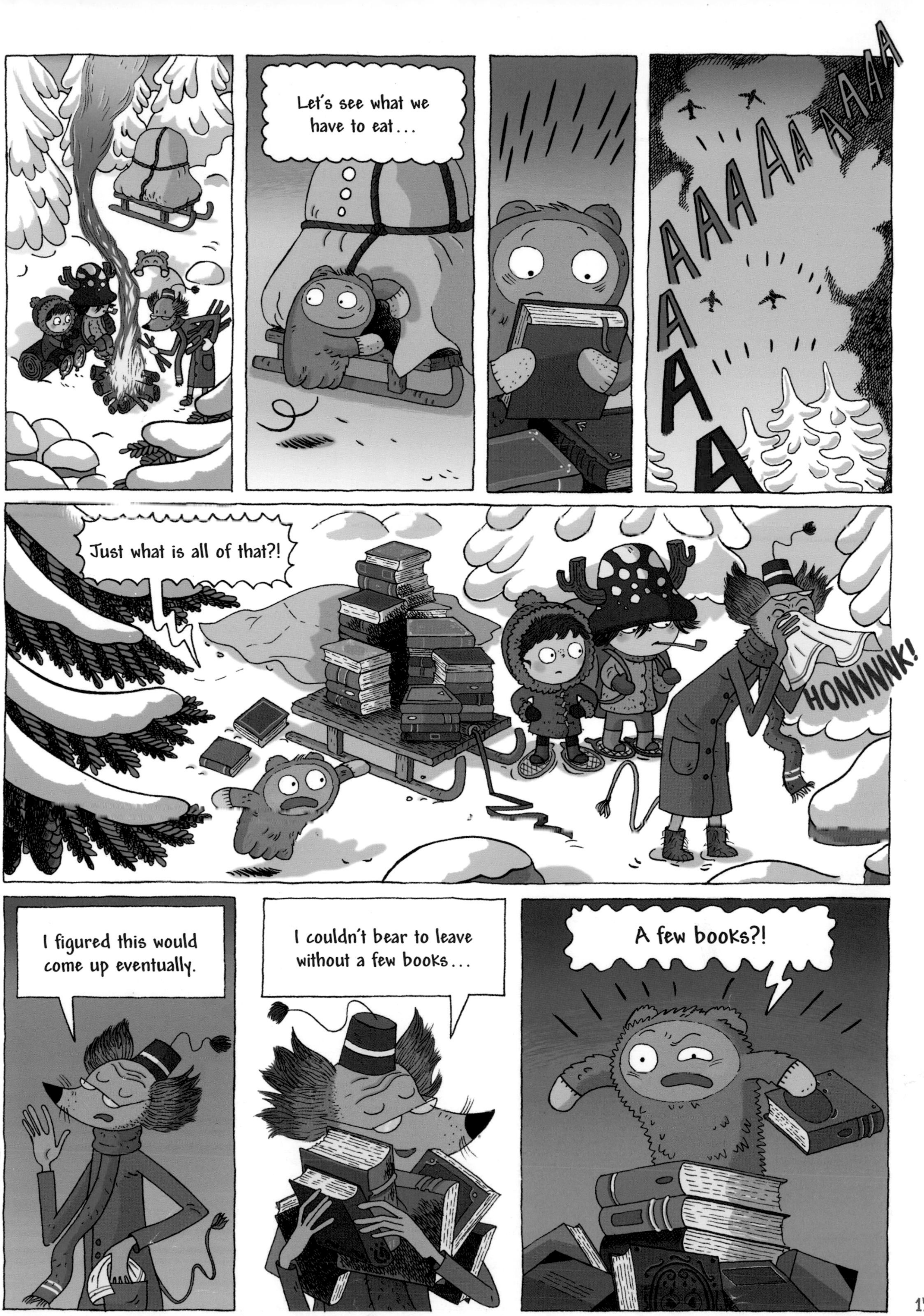
Let's see what we have to eat...
AAAAAAAAAAAAAAA
Just what is all of that?!
HONNNNK!
I figured this would come up eventually.
I couldn't bear to leave without a few books...
A few books?!

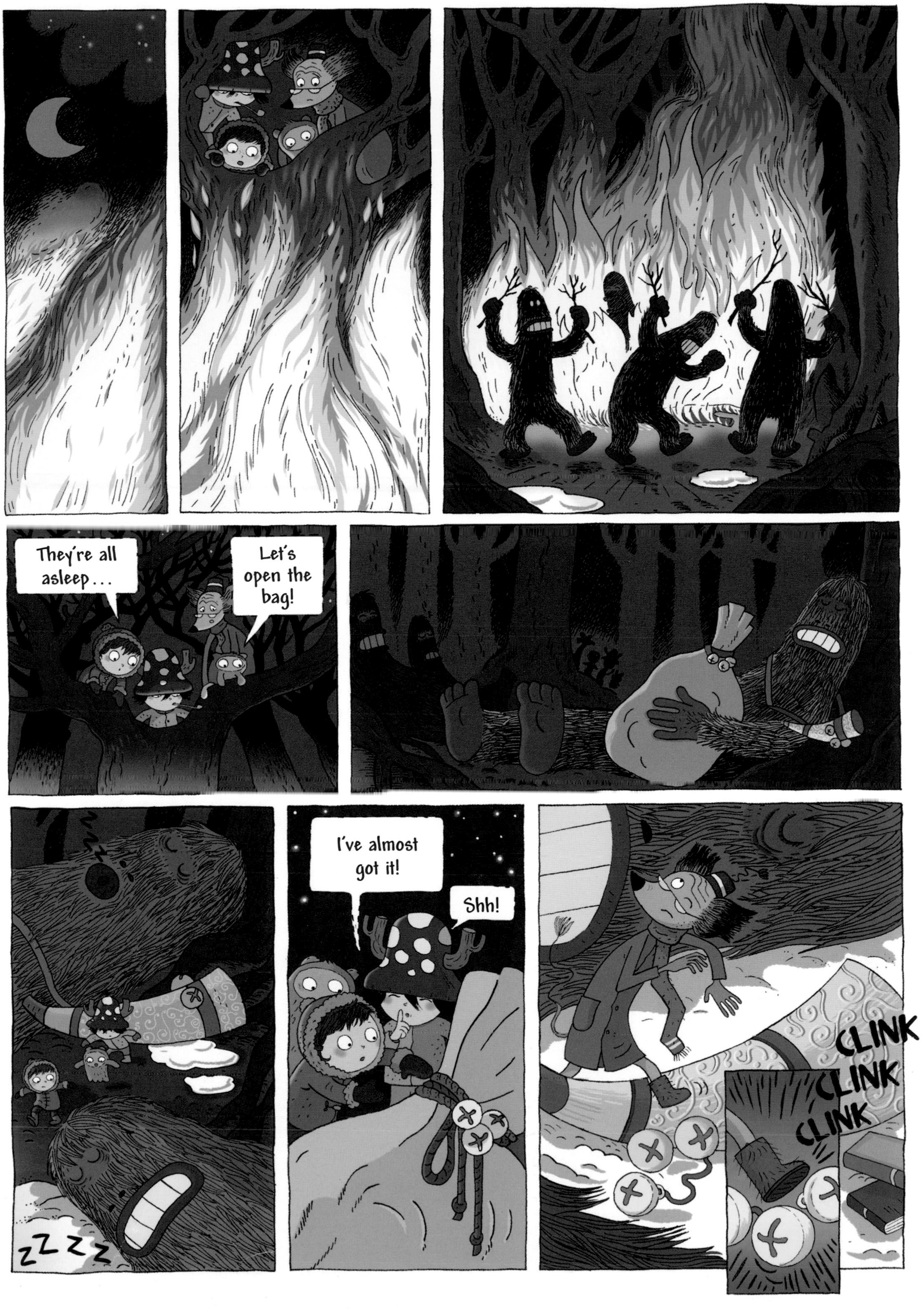
They're all asleep...
Let's open the bag!
ZZZZ
I've almost got it!
Shh!
CLINK
CLINK
CLINK

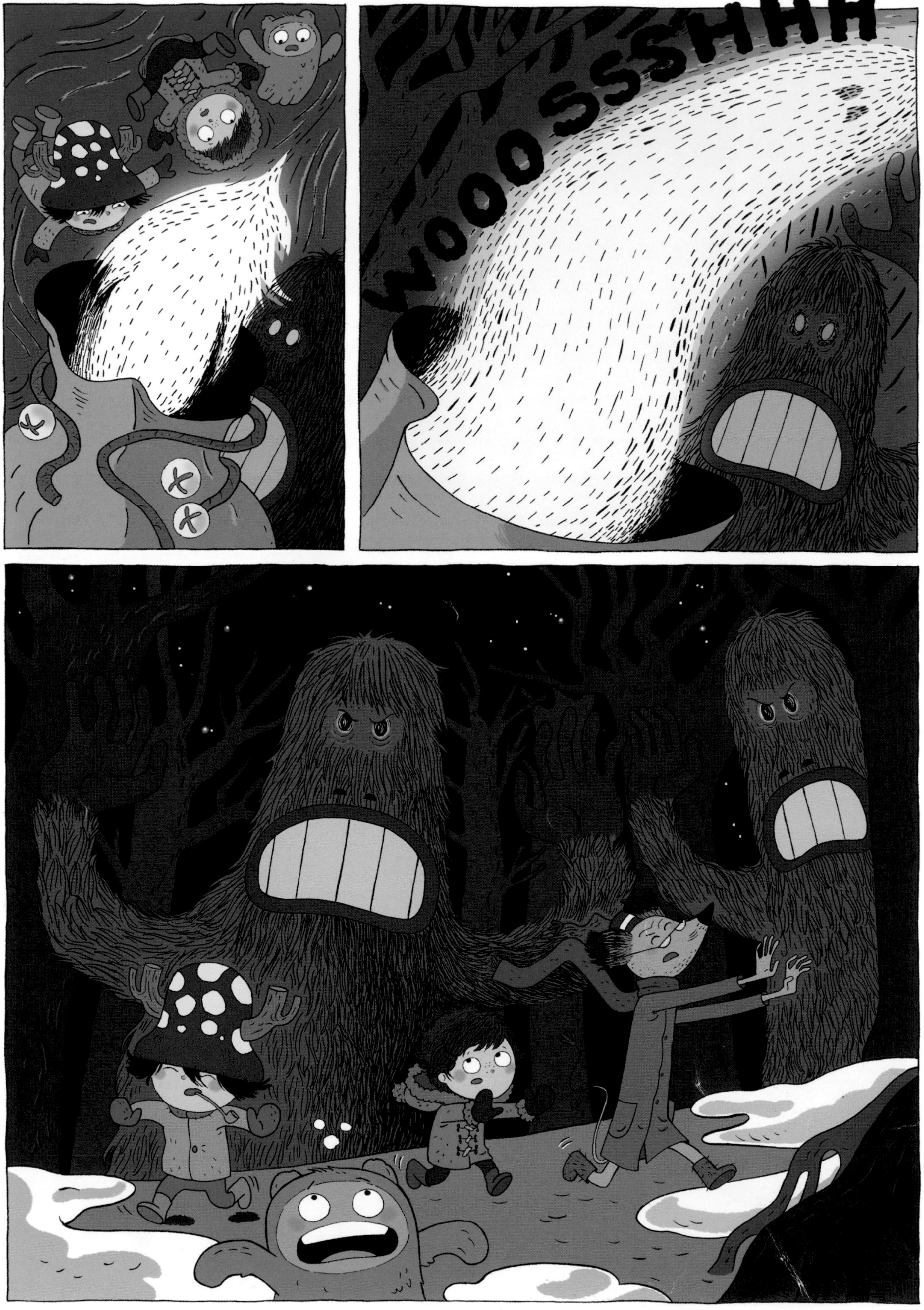
WOOOSSSHHH

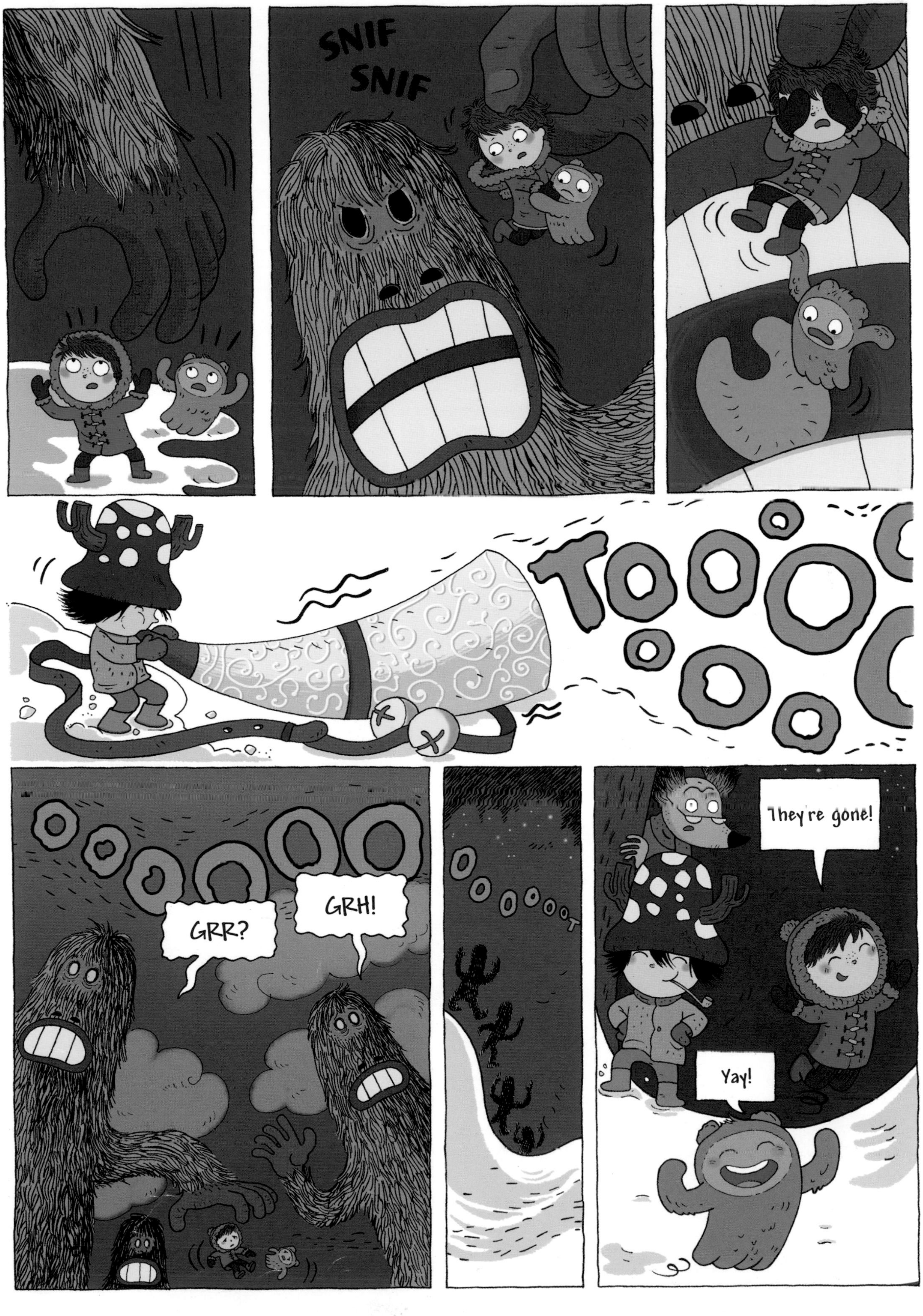
SNIF
SNIF
TOOOOOOO
OOOOOOO
GRR?
GRH!
OOOOOOOT
They're gone!
Yay!

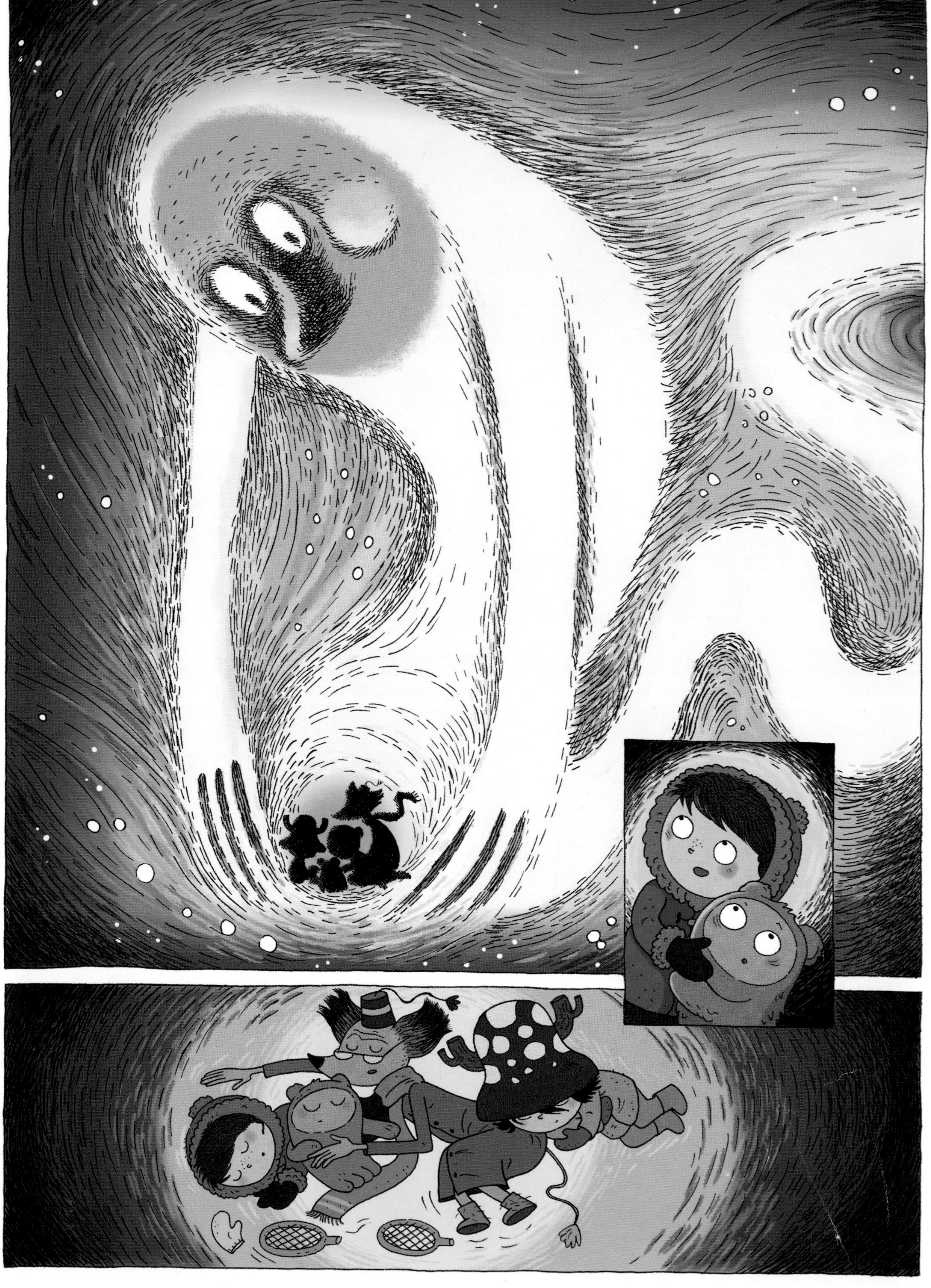

33

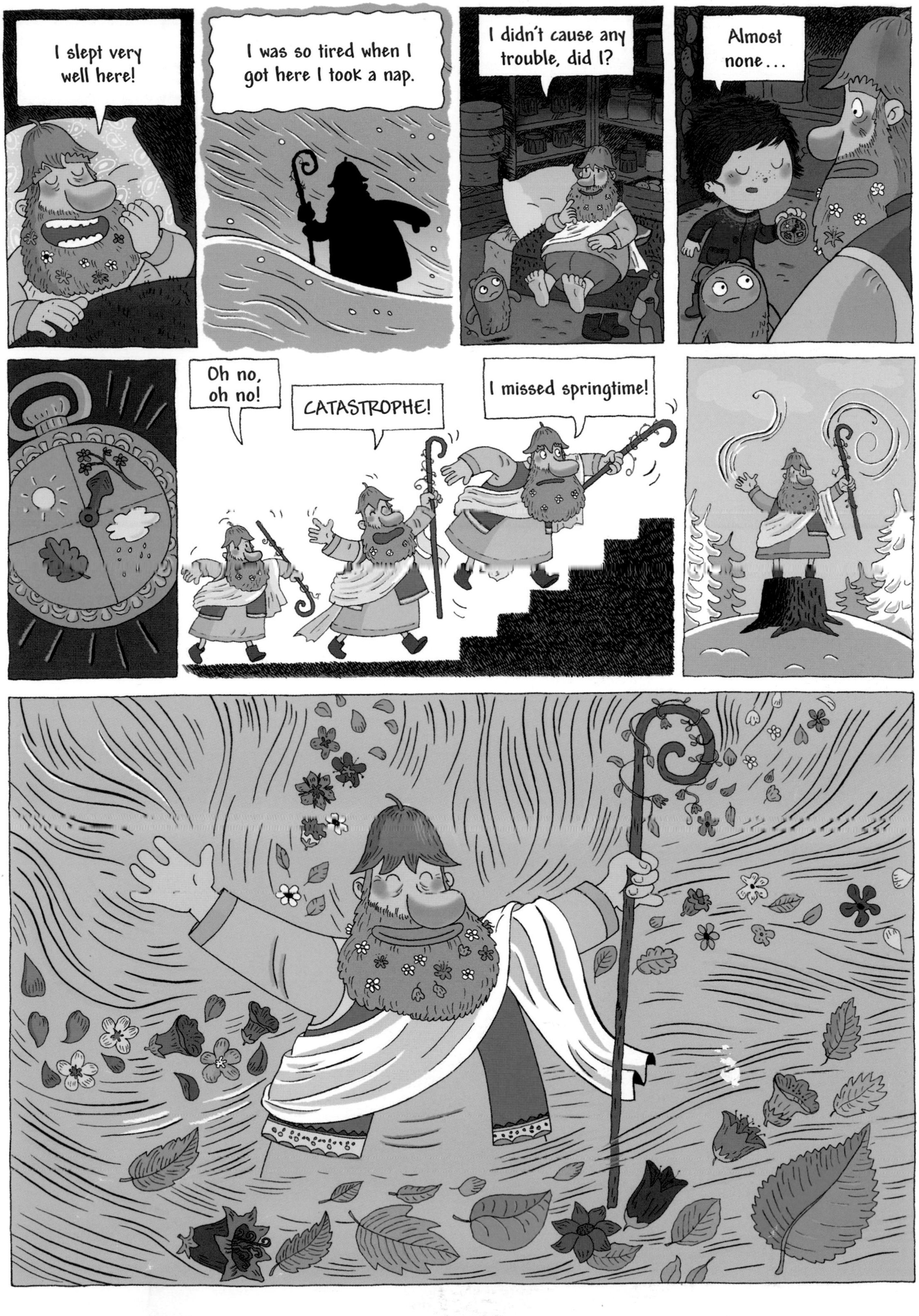
I slept very well here!
I was so tired when I got here I took a nap.
I didn't cause any trouble, did I?
Almost none...
Oh no, oh no!
CATASTROPHE!
I missed springtime!

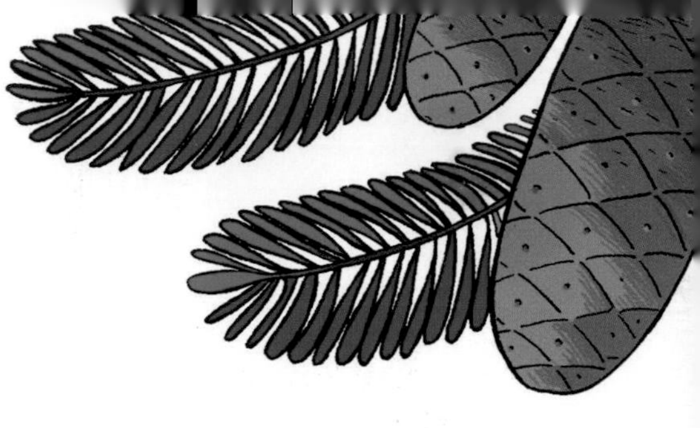

Sponge Cake

Ask an adult for help in the kitchen.

7 tablespoons butter
$\frac{1}{2}$ cup flour
$\frac{3}{4}$ cup granulated sugar
$\frac{1}{2}$ cup almond meal (also known as almond flour)
1 pinch salt
4 egg whites

preparation time: 15 minutes
cooking time: 20 to 25 minutes

1. Preheat the oven to 350°F. Line the cups of a standard 12-cup muffin pan with paper liners.
2. Melt butter in a small pan until it just starts to brown, approximately 3 to 5 minutes. Let cool.
3. Stir together flour, sugar, almond meal, and salt.
4. Use a hand mixer or a stand mixer to beat butter and egg whites into the flour mixture. Beat for 1 to 2 minutes to fully blend the ingredients.
5. Divide the mixture evenly among the prepared muffin cups—filling them one-half to three-quarters full. Place the muffin pan in the oven. Let cook 20 to 25 minutes until the sponge cakes have browned.
6. Let the sponge cakes cool slightly, 1 to 2 minutes. Then gently turn them out of the pans and let them cool the rest of the way on a cooling rack.

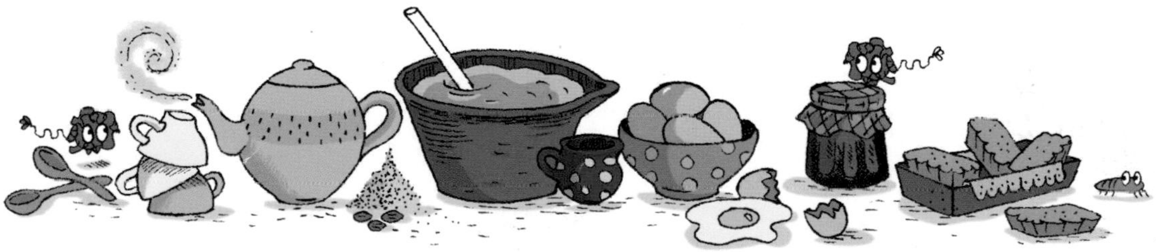

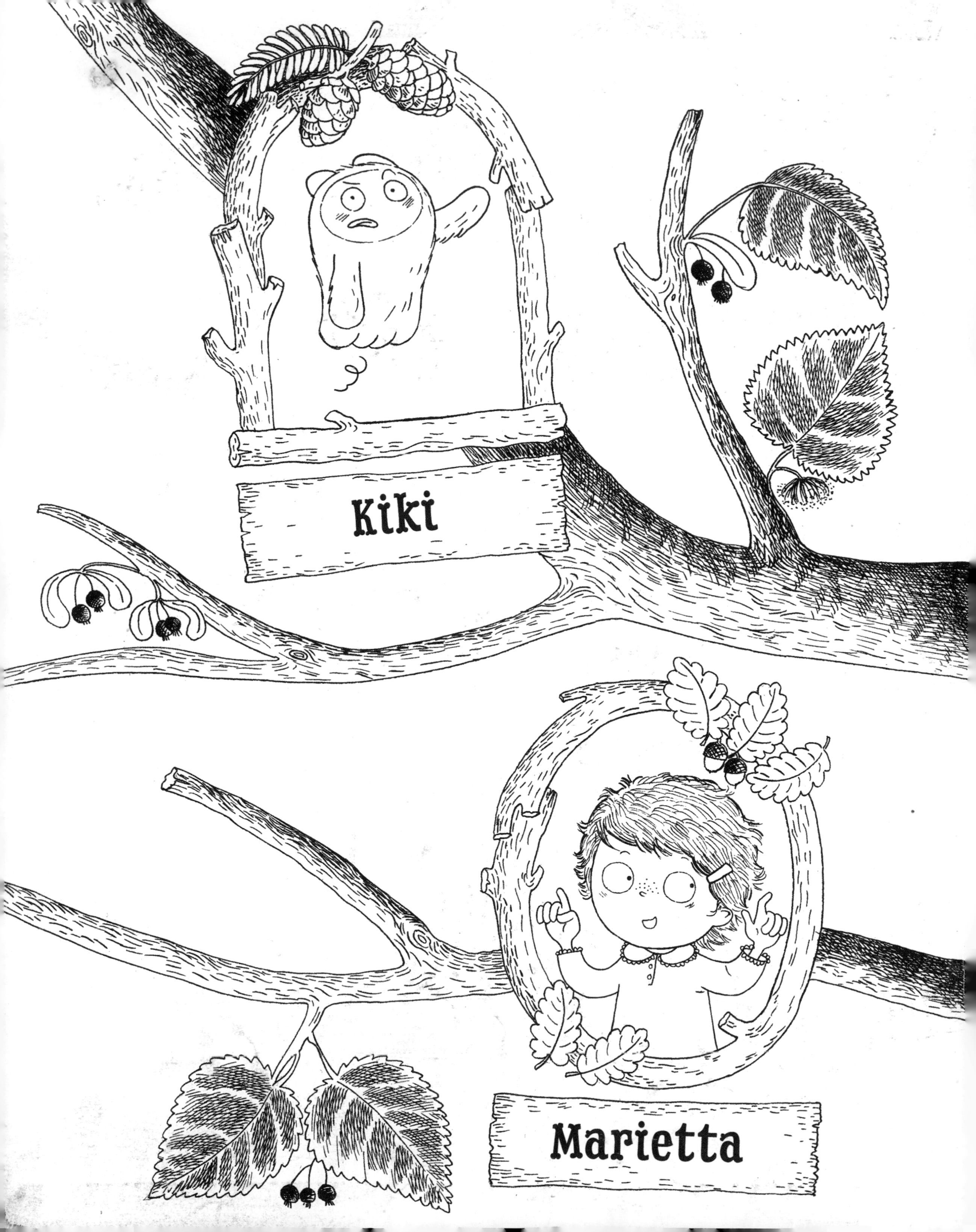
Kiki
Marietta